The Boy at the Park

Story by Carmel Reilly

Illustrations by Pat Reynolds

Contents

HOUGHTON MIFFLIN HARCOURT
Supplemental Publishers

www.Rigby.com
800-531-5015

Chapter 1

The Chalk Drawing

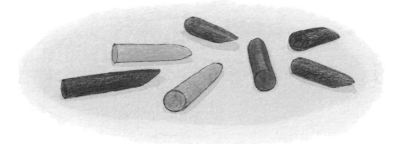

Nina and Eddie had come to the park
to play basketball.
As they walked toward the basketball court,
Nina pointed to a boy who was crouched down
on the pavement nearby.

"What's that boy doing?" she asked.

When Nina and Eddie came closer,
they could see that he was drawing
a picture of someone playing basketball.

"That's a great picture," Nina said to the boy.

The boy shrugged, but he didn't turn around.

"It must have taken a long time to draw it," said Eddie.

The boy didn't answer.

Eddie and Nina looked at each other, and then they ran onto the court.

Eddie took a shot at the basket, but he threw the ball too hard and it flew past the hoop.

"Oh, no!" Nina said with a gasp.

The ball sailed toward the boy
and landed right on his drawing.

Chapter 2

It Was an Accident!

"I'm sorry!" shouted Eddie.

But the boy didn't look at Eddie.
He jumped up, grabbed the ball,
and threw it into the bushes.

"I'm sorry!" Eddie said again
as he ran past the boy to get the ball.
"I really didn't mean to hit your drawing."

Nina walked over. "Hey," she said.
"You didn't need to throw our ball over there.
Eddie said he was sorry."

The boy looked up at her.
"I've worked hard on this drawing," he said.

Nina frowned and said, "It was an accident!"
But the boy turned away and didn't answer her.

Nina and Eddie picked up their ball and went back to playing.

After a few minutes, the boy got up and started walking toward them.

"He might be coming to say he's sorry,"
said Eddie.

"I don't think so," said Nina
when she saw the look on the boy's face.

Chapter 3
Quick Moves

Suddenly, the boy ran straight toward Eddie and grabbed the ball out of his hands.

He bounced the ball down the court.

"I'll show you how basketball should be played!" the boy yelled.
"My dad used to be a champion player and he taught me."

"Here," called Eddie. "Pass the ball back."

The boy laughed.
"You come and get it if you can," he said.

"Please," said Nina, "if you want to play with us, you have to play by the rules."

"Who said so?" the boy yelled.
Then he ran down the court.

Chapter 4

The Champion Player

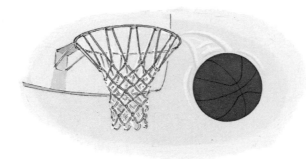

The boy tried to shoot a basket,
but suddenly Eddie appeared right beside him.

As the ball fell back toward him,
Eddie jumped up and grabbed it.

He raced down the court with the ball.

The boy followed him, trying as hard as he could
to snatch the ball back.

"Now you're not being fair!" said the boy.

"Yes, he is," said Nina.
"You're just annoyed that he's better than you!"

Suddenly, someone called out, "Dylan!"

A man walked toward them.
"Dylan, it's time to go," he said.

"Coming, Dad," Dylan called back.

Eddie stared at the man.
He knew he had seen him somewhere before.

"My dad used to play for the City Superstars,"
said Dylan. "I told you he was famous.
One day I'll be a famous player
for the City Superstars, too."

"That's the team I want to be on!"
said Eddie.

Dylan's father looked at Eddie.
"I'm sure that you'll be a City Superstars player
one of these days, young man.
I've been watching you,
and you are already a good player.
You never know," he said, laughing.
"You and Dylan might even end up
on the same team one day."